# The Teddy Bears' Picnic

*Pictures by*
**Prue Theobalds**

*Words by*
**Jimmy Kennedy**

**Blackie**
London

**Bedrick/Blackie**
New York

If you go down in the woods today
You're sure of a big surprise.

If you go down in the woods today
You'd better go in disguise;

For ev'ry Bear that ever there was
Will gather there for certain, because
Today's the day the Teddy Bears have their picnic.

Ev'ry Teddy Bear who's been good
Is sure of a treat today.

There's lots of marvellous things to eat,

And wonderful games to play.

Beneath the trees where nobody sees
They'll hide and seek as long as they please,
'Cause that's the way the Teddy Bears have their picnic.

If you go down in the woods today
You'd better not go alone.

It's lovely down in the woods today
But safer to stay at home.

For ev'ry Bear that ever there was

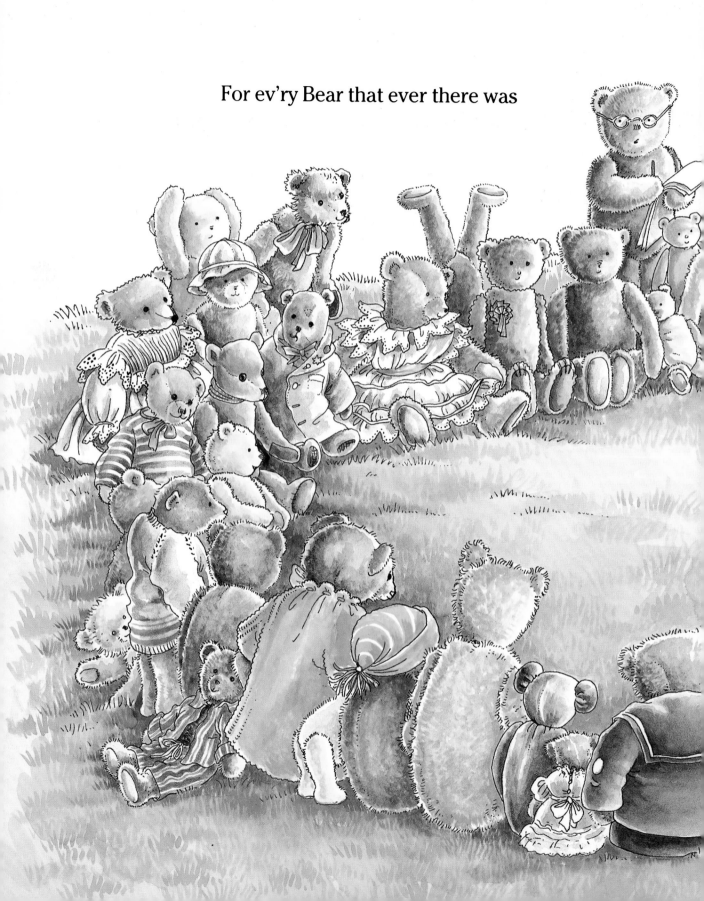

Will gather there for certain, because
Today's the day the Teddy Bears have their picnic.

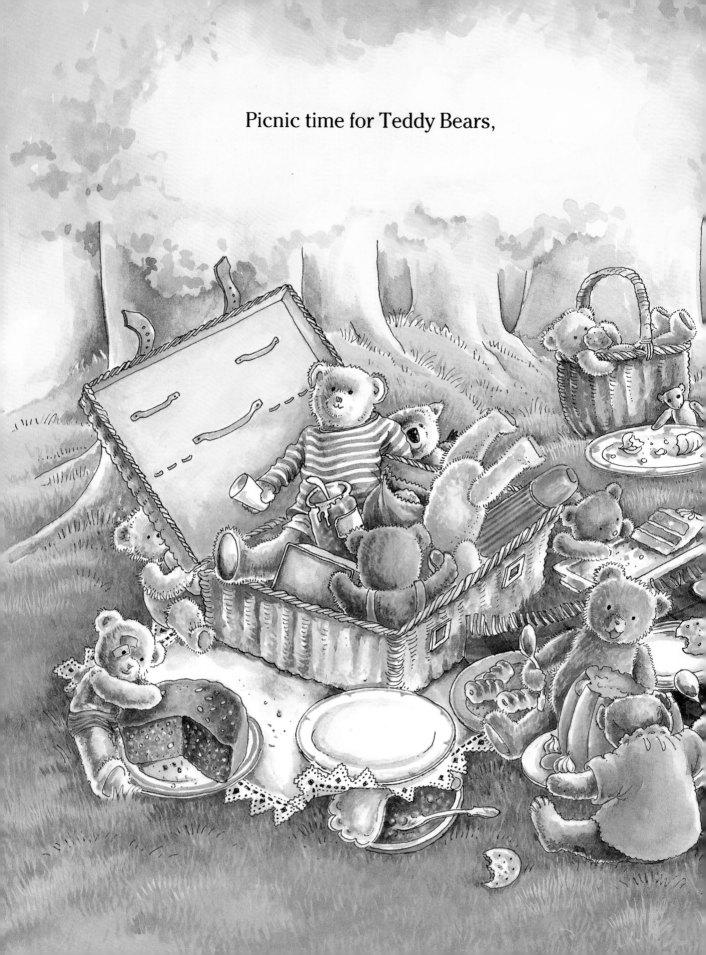

Picnic time for Teddy Bears,

The little Teddy Bears are having a lovely time today.
Watch them, catch them unawares
And see them picnic on their holiday.

See them gaily gad about,
They love to play and shout;
They never have any care;

At six o'clock their Mummies and Daddies
Will take them home to bed,
Because they're tired little Teddy Bears.

For
*Tubby-toes, Hawthorn and Pteddy*
who all like picnics

*The artist would like to thank*
*The Bethnal Green Museum of Childhood,*
*Arundel Toy and Military Museum*
*and the Bear Museum, Petersfield*
*for the inspiration for many of the*
*bears portrayed in this book.*

BLACKIE CHILDREN'S BOOKS
Penguin Books, Harmondsworth, Middlesex, England
Australia, Canada, New Zealand

*First published 1987 by*
Blackie and Son Ltd.,
*Reprinted 1992 by*
Blackie Children's Books
27 Wrights Lane
LONDON W8 5TZ

*This edition published 1992 by*
Peter Bedrick Books
2112 Broadway, New York, NY 10023

*Text of the Song 'The Teddy Bears' Picnic'*
Copyright © 1932 B. Feldman and Co. Ltd.,
London WC2H 0LD.
*Reproduced by permission of EMI Music Publishing Ltd*
*and International Music Publications*

*'The Teddy Bears' Picnic'* words by Jimmy Kennedy
Copyright © 1907 and 1947 Warner Bros. Inc. Copyright renewed
*Used by permission*

Illustrations copyright © 1987 Prue Theobalds

British Library Cataloguing in Publication Data
Kennedy, Jimmy
   The teddy bears' picnic.
   I. Title    II. Theobalds, Prue
823'.914[J]    PZ7
ISBN 0-216-92097-3
ISBN 0-216-92270-4 Pbk

Library of Congress Cataloging-in-Publication Data.
Kennedy, Jimmy.
   The teddy bears' picnic.
   Summary: presents the texts of the familiar song
   about the festivities at the teddy-bears'-picnic
   1. Children's song    2. Text.    1. Teddy bears — poetry.
   2. Picknicking — poetry.    3. Songs
   I. Theobalds.    Prue, ill.    II. Title
   PZ8.3.K383Te 1987    [E]    86-32111

   ISBN 0-87226-153-0   ISBN 0-87226-424-6 (pbk.)

*Printed in Hong Kong by Wing King Tong Co Ltd*